nickelodeon

PAW PATROL™

See & Say Storybook

Pups Save Friendship Day!

To Zuma

To Skye

PaRRagon

Bath · New York · Cologne · Melbourne · Delhi
Hong Kong · Shenzhen · Singapore

How to use this book

This See & Say storybook replaces key words with pictures. It encourages children to begin reading aloud, and makes sharing stories even more fun.

Read the *PAW Patrol* story together and wherever a picture appears, look back at the picture glossary page to discover what the word should be.

For example: = balloons

Some pictures have been repeated several times within the story. As children begin to recognize the pictures, their reading confidence will improve and they may no longer need to look back at the picture glossary.

Picture glossary

 Balloons

 Baskets

 Bunnies

 Cake

 Cards

 Chase

 Fire engine

 Kittens

 Ladder

 Marshall

 Mayor Goodway

 Mayor Humdinger

 Mr Postman

 Rocky

 Rubble

 Ryder

 Skye

 Digger

 Zuma

 and the PAW Patrol pups were in the Lookout getting

ready for Friendship Day.  flew up high and helped

 and hang decorations.

squirted paint to make lots of friendship  .

 put the  in envelopes while licked

stamps and stuck them on. Soon everything was finished and

the pups were ready to take the  to  . He would

deliver the to all their friends in Adventure Bay.

 helped load the friendship

into his yellow  and off they went to find  .

On the way, they drove past a scary old house.

 and  heard creepy scratching sounds and

drove away as fast as they could.

The pups soon found  . He was delighted to deliver

the friendship . was also pleased. She wanted

Adventure Bay to be the friendliest town around.

But  and the Kit-tastrophe Crew had been making

, too. wanted his town, Foggy Bottom,

to be the friendliest town.

 said they should have a contest. The town with

the best Friendship Day gift would win. But one of the

 started firing  at 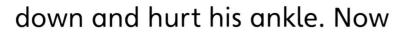 . He fell

down and hurt his ankle. Now  couldn't make any

deliveries at all!

needed the PAW Patrol's help to deliver the

 , so called the pups on his PupPad.

 flew above Adventure Bay dropping

 as she went, while sped out to sea in

his hovercraft giving  to the creatures there.

 needed his  with a to make some

tricky deliveries. Hootie Owl lived in a tall tree, so

climbed up his to reach her. But on his way up he

slipped and fell, and the friendship  fell right

into the garden of the scary house!

 was also doing an important job.  had made

the tallest Friendship Day ever! sped off in his

police truck to deliver the to  .

But was busy with his own Friendship Day gifts.

He was preparing full of sweets for everyone in

Adventure Bay. The cheeky  tied to

the .

It wasn't long before heard about the giant .

He couldn't let win the contest!

Sneakily, threw pins onto the road and when

drove over them in his police truck, the air came hissing out

of his tyres. When came to a stop, the started to

topple over until it was a terrible mess. Now couldn't

deliver the at all! watched from behind a tree

and smiled – his plan was working!

But 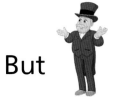 didn't realise that there was a small problem

with his gifts.... Some were tempted by the

delicious sweets in the ! They climbed inside just

as the lifted the off the ground. Now the air

was full of floating !

 gently guided the  towards ,

who launched tennis balls to pop the . Soon, all of

the  were safely back on the ground again. Phew!

When realized that the  had eaten all his sweets,

he was very angry. But he soon came up with a new plan.

He gathered together all of the and presented

them to  as a Friendship Day gift. But poor didn't

have a gift to give in return! It looked like  was going

to win the contest after all.

Just then, and drove up with the most amazing

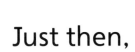 anyone had ever seen. Clever had used the

spatula tool in his Pup Pack to make the  look like !

Even the Kit-tastrophe had to admit that it was a

very handsome .

 sighed. His plan had failed. Now  and

were sure that Adventure Bay would be known as

the friendliest town of all.

Back at the scary house, was out of the tree,

but the  were still in the garden. With

by his side, bravely went to get the  back.

But the lady who lived in the house wasn't scary at all.

Her name was Miss Marjorie, and it was her pet raccoon,

Maynard, who had made the scratching sounds!

Miss Marjorie was happy to see and .

She didn't get many visitors because people were scared

of her house.

 and were pleased to invite their new friends to

the Friendship Day party. While and  delivered the

last of the friendship 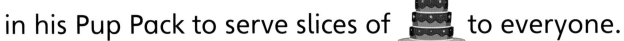, used the claw

in his Pup Pack to serve slices of  to everyone.

Even and 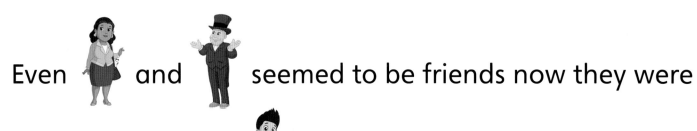 seemed to be friends now they were

back on the ground! 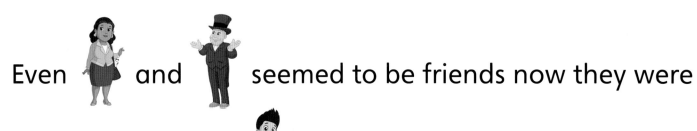 was so proud of his clever pups.

What a perfect way to celebrate Friendship Day, with both

old and new friends.